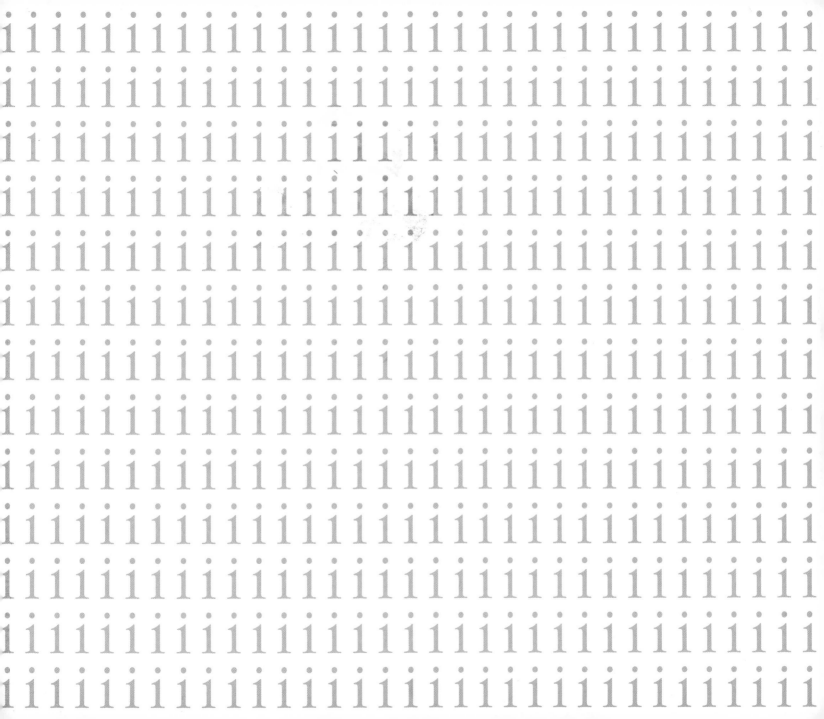

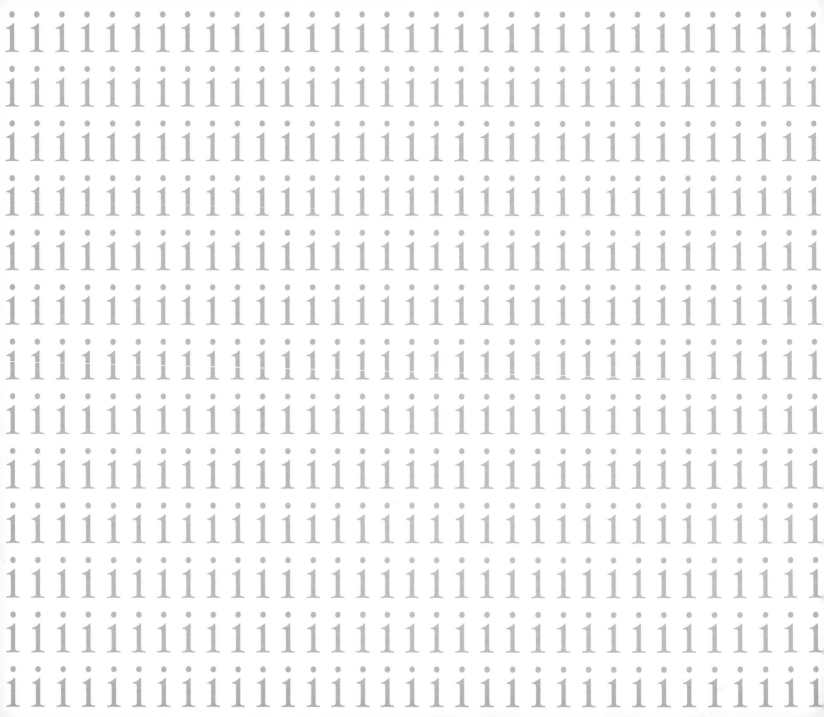

My "i" Sound Box®

(This book concentrates on the short "i" sound in the story line. Words beginning with the long "i" sound are included at the end of the book.)

Library of Congress Cataloging-in-Publication Data
Moncure, Jane Belk.
My "i" sound box / by Jane Belk Moncure; illustrated by Colin King.
p. cm.
Summary: A little girl fills her sound box with many words beginning with the letter "i."
ISBN 1-56766-775-9 (lib. reinforced : alk. paper)
[1. Alphabet.] I. King, Colin, ill. II. Title.
PZ7.M739 Myi   2000
[E]—dc21   99-056559

My "i" Sound Box

Jane Belk Moncure

illustrated by Colin King

The Child's World

Little  had a box.

"I will find things that begin with my 'i' sound," she said.

"I will put them into my sound box."

Little went skip, skip, skip up a hill.

She found inchworms,

lots of inchworms.

The inchworms wiggled and wiggled.

"What wiggly inchworms," she said.

Did she put the inchworms
into her box? She did.

Then Little  found iguanas,

lots of iguanas.

The iguanas wiggled and wiggled.

"What wiggly iguanas," she said.

She put the iguanas into the box
with the inchworms.

But the inchworms did not like
the iguanas!

The inchworms jumped out of the box.

The iguanas jumped, too.

Away they went!

Little i could not find

the inchworms or . . .

the iguanas.

They were hiding.

Then Little

found an igloo.

Did she put the igloo into her box?
She did.

Just then, the sun came out.
Guess what?

The igloo melted.

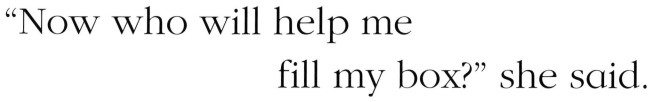

"Now who will help me
fill my box?" she said.

A friend came by.

"I will help you," he said.

"We can fill your box with insects."

First they found big green insects.

Lots of big green insects.

Next they found yellow insects and brown insects.

Then they found red and black insects.
"What else can we do?' said Little

"We can make an insect zoo."
You can visit it, too.

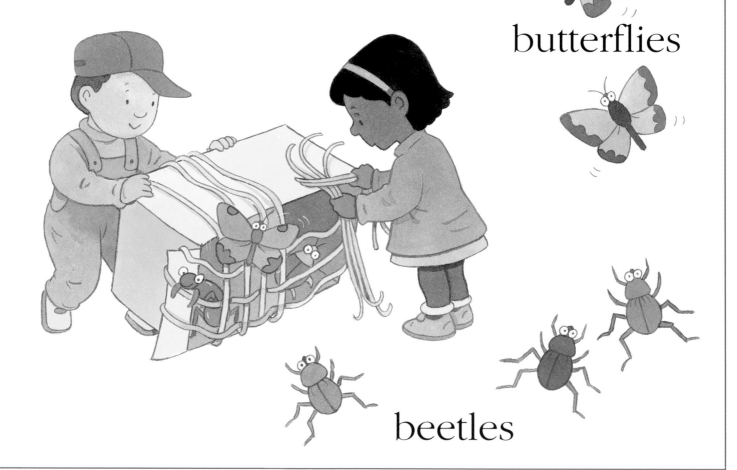

butterflies

beetles

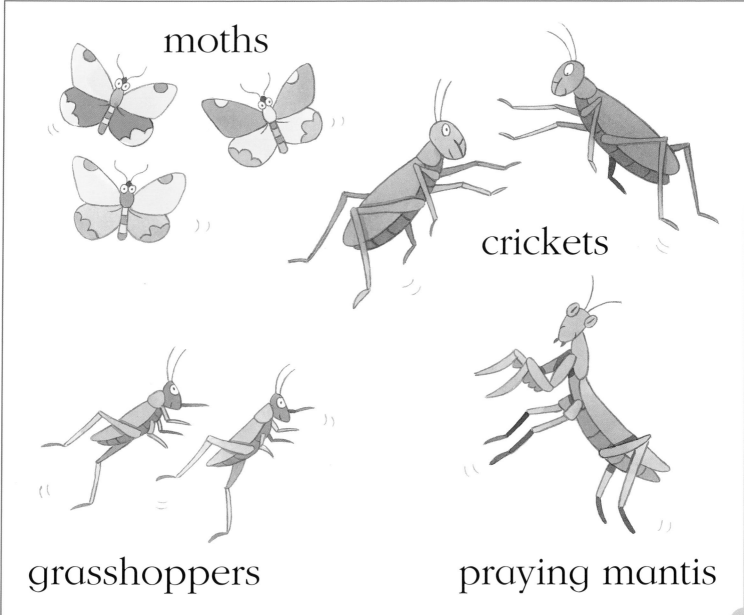

moths

crickets

grasshoppers

praying mantis

Can you read these words
with Little  ?

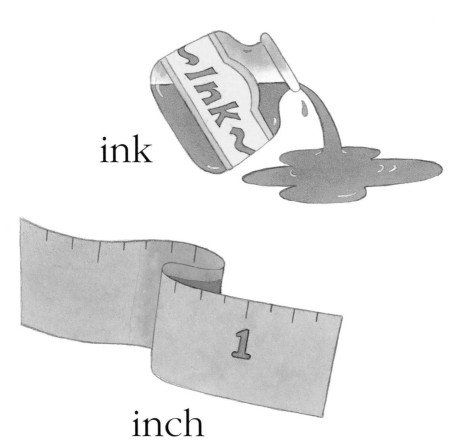

ink

inch

infant

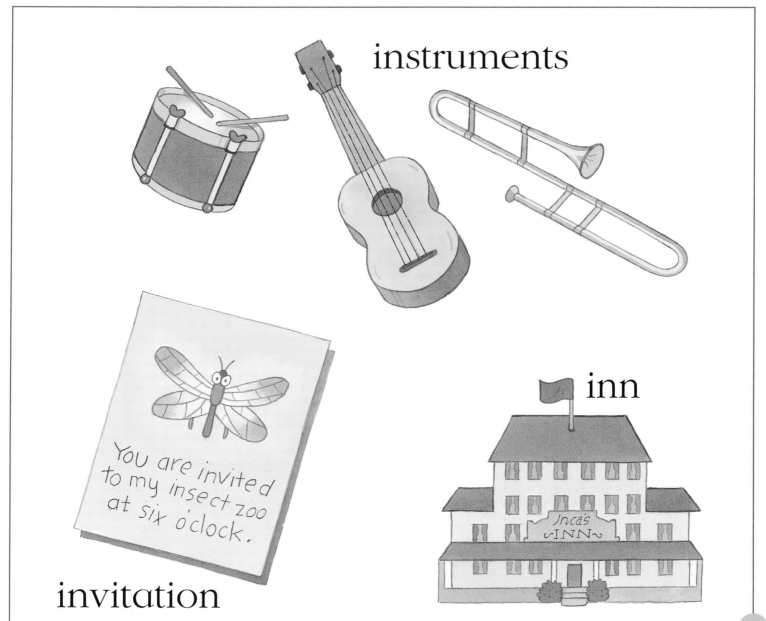

instruments

inn

You are invited to my insect zoo at six o'clock.

invitation

Inca's INN

29

Little  has another sound in some words. She says her name, "i."

Can you read these words?
Listen for Little 's name.

ice cubes

ice cream

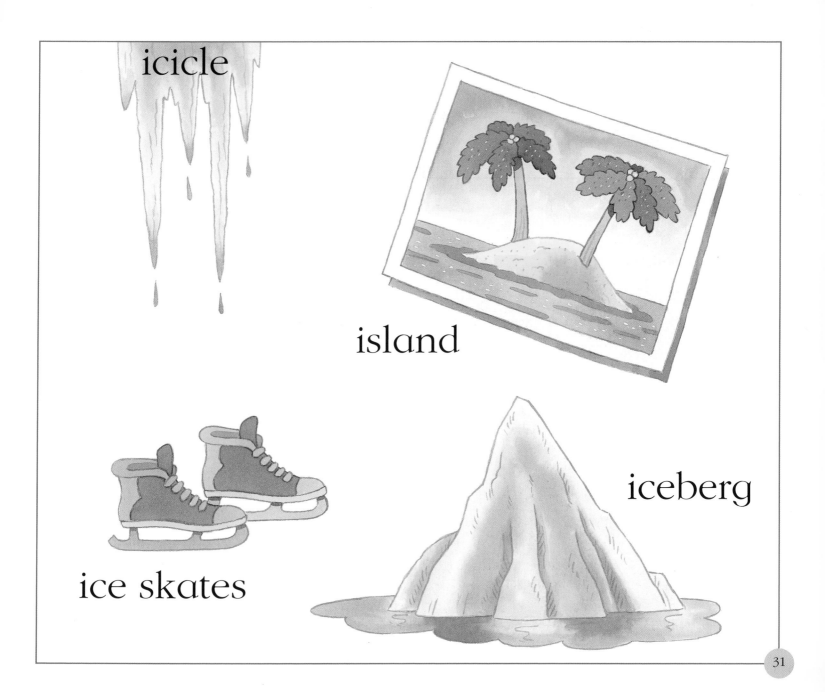

icicle

island

ice skates

iceberg

ABOUT THE AUTHOR AND ILLUSTRATOR

Jane Belk Moncure began her writing career when she was in kindergarten. She has never stopped writing. Many of her children's stories and poems have been published, to the delight of young readers, including her son Jim, whose childhood experiences found their way into many of her books.

Mrs. Moncure's writing is based upon an active career in early childhood education. A recipient of an M.A. degree from Columbia University, Mrs. Moncure has taught and directed nursery, kindergarten, and primary grade programs in California, New York, Virginia, and North Carolina. As a former member of the faculties of Virginia Commonwealth University and the University of Richmond, she taught prospective teachers in early childhood education.

Mrs. Moncure has travelled extensively abroad, studying early childhood programs in the United Kingdom, The Netherlands, and Switzerland. She was the first president of the Virginia Association for Early Childhood Education and received its award for outstanding service to young children.

A resident of North Carolina, Mrs. Moncure is currently a full-time writer and educational consultant. She is married to Dr. James A. Moncure, former vice president of Elon College.

Colin King studied at the Royal College of Art, London. He started his freelance career as an illustrator, working for magazines and advertising agencies.

He began drawing pictures for children's books in 1976 and has illustrated over sixty titles to date.

Included in a wide variety of subjects are a best-selling children's encyclopedia and books about spies and detectives.

His books have been translated into several languages, including Japanese and Hebrew. He has four grown-up children and lives in Suffolk, England, with his wife, three dogs, and a cat.